DEER HEAD

KAYIN VAN NELSON

A catalogue record for this work is available from the National Library of Australia

National Library of Australia Catalogue-in-Publication data:
Deer Head/Kayin Van Nelson

ISBN: 978-0-6451484-0-4
(Paperback)

ISBN: 978-0-6451483-7-4
(eBook)

"From there we came outside and saw the stars"
— **Dante Alighieri, Inferno**

THE WAGON ROCKS AND ROLLS as the horses trot up the hill. An old stone wall covered in moss follows alongside the gravel path. Several times the wagon lurches threateningly toward the wall, but the pair never meet. At the crest of the hill, an ancient angel oak tree awaits their arrival. Its tentacle branches snake across the sky like a spider perched against the wall of heaven. A bad omen to most travellers, but the folk in this wagon pay it no heed.

The twang of a mandolin, plucked by delicate fingers, rings out across the weathered landscape. The high-pitched wail of a harmonica soon joins it. A painful tune of hope and redemption that bruises the senses. The horses stop, and the wagon shudders to a halt; the animals cock their heads to the music. The Driver, seated at the front of the wagon, has no choice but to flick her whip, prompting the horses to neigh in frustration and continue trudging up the hill.

Inside the wagon, the passengers clap their hands and tap their feet to the shifting beat of the music. The two players – a stout man with the absurdly small mandolin cradled in his arms and a square-shouldered Brute with the harmonica held tightly between his lips – shake and move their bodies as though they are possessed.

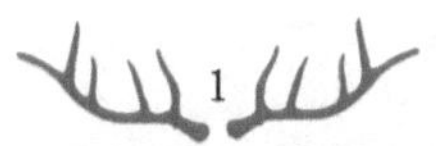

Around them, the tarp roofing of the wagon ripples in the early winter winds.

DAYLIGHT FADES INTO OBSCURITY AS the moon gleams and the sun sinks underground, to wherever it may slumber. The wagon is beneath the oak tree, the horses untied and absently clearing away the grass. The others, two men and three women (not including The Driver, who is nowhere to be seen), are pitching the tents. The unshaven Brute watches them from the stone wall encasing the camp, where he cleans out the barrel of his rifle.

He's been chewing tobacco – not out of choice – but now spits it onto the ground. His wide-brimmed hat feels heavier than usual, an anchor weighing him down. He takes it off and places it beside him, letting his hair fall into his eyes. He misses home, more now than ever. He will make them pay for what they did, for forcing him to leave his life behind. He tries not to think about the flames hot against his skin or the smoke stinging his eyes. Even in those final moments, the house was beautiful.

Still scrubbing away at the gun, The Brute flicks his eyes to the moon, a pearly white coin in a fountain of black water. According to his mother, in the old days, thieves would steal the moon and wish upon it with greed gnawing on their minds, but heroes brought those thieves to justice and placed the moon back in its rightful place.

The Brute hates this place, these people; they know him too well and hate him too little. There's no blame from himself or from others and now, his sins are fading. By next Friday they will be dead and forgotten. The Brute wishes judgement day would come and cast him into hell's pits. He looks back up at the moon, how easy it would be to pluck the thing from the sky, to see more clearly while the rest went blind. One wish wouldn't hurt anybody.

***

CLEAN RIFLE SLUNG ACROSS HIS back. Tobacco trapped between his gums and inner cheek, jaw constantly at work chewing it. Hat tilted slightly upward, light twinkling in his soft green eyes. Boots trudging through the slush of melted snow that fell late last night. Icicles dangling everywhere, rattling in the wind, under constant threat of shattering. Birds sailing onto trees, sending the resting snow on branches crashing down, disturbing the wildlife. The hunt has begun.

The Driver, short and slender as she is, capably glides over the snow, twirling her hunting knife between her fingers. She's the only one of the travellers who agreed to accompany The Brute. He has never seen The Driver hunt, barely knows the woman to be honest. But the look in her eyes – like a lone tree amid a wildfire, immune to all of Mother Nature's power – tells The Brute that he has little to fear.

They ran out of food three days ago and have been hunting ever since. Up until today, there'd been no sign of game. Then this morning, after the snow, they found two sets of tracks. The Brute reasons one set could be deer, based on the shape and depth of the footprints. The other set is unclear, though it's far heavier and larger. The Driver claims the sudden snow is a miracle from God. The Brute is not a religious man, but staring up at the cold sun, its absence against his bleached skin, he can't help but wonder if The Driver is right.

In a gap between the pine trees, The Brute sights the deer. It's standing at the top of a pile of rocks, a heavenly glow slipping between the trees behind it, almost godlike. Without hesitation, The Brute aims down the sights of his rifle; it's the perfect shot. The Driver shouts something he doesn't hear and then the roar of a minotaur – or some equally disturbing monster – erupts beside him. He turns and sees a beast with fire for fur and jaws wider than a canyon.

It barrels toward him with the speed and power of a steam train.

The Brute swings his gun toward it too late and the demonic creature reaches him. Darkness encompasses the world.

***

He is in a cabin. The walls are damp wood and the floor creaks wherever he steps. The fireplace is empty, save for grey ash, and all the lights are off. Dust hangs suspended in the air, making him cough. In front of him, stitched to a plaque, is the stuffed head of a deer. Its eyes are wide and afraid. Beneath it, in gold scrawl; Ad Meliora.

He glances through the window; outside are rolling hills covered in flowers of all kinds. Purple and white lilies, yellow tulips, red dahlias. Doves float through the cloudless sky, completely carefree. Someone else is out in the meadow, a young girl. She's picking flowers; her hair is a curly storm. He can't see her face, but something about her fills him with dread. He is a rain-filled cloud ready to burst.

He returns his attention to the cabin, only to find the deer head has caught on fire. He can feel the animal's spirit soaking into his bones. The fire trickles down the wall and into the fireplace, where it roars into growling life. The inferno is goading him toward it, but The Brute resists. The flames angrily blaze into an impenetrable wall that crashes toward him. He dives for the door but the fire is already inside him; it burns his insides.

He bursts into the peaceful countryside, alarming a flock of starling birds, only to find his wool coat is alight and cackling. He drops and rolls, but the fire wraps around his body, enveloping him in a bear hug. The cabin in front of him crumbles, the wood splinters and the roof caves in on itself. The Brute lets the fire consume him.

Up in the great beyond, an orange disc shimmers as it hovers

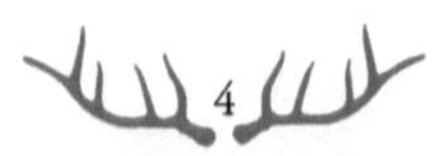

above the clouds, a faceless angel. The sun! A force radiates from it. Beckoning him closer. His body is stuck to the ground, and up-turned roots dig into his back. A rabbit edges closer. Is it curious of the burning man or in desperate need of warmth?

The sun is the moon's father, it is the opposing side of the same coin. Hiding. Where the moon is maternal, nurturing the waves, the sun abandons in the night and kills in the day. No one has ever wished upon the sun like they have the moon, for fear of being burned. But The Brute is already on fire: What harm could it do?

***

THE DRIVER THRUSTS A KNIFE deep into the beast's red eye, making the veins pop out like flashes of lightning. The Brute blinks away the hallucination and realises the demonic creature is, in fact, an enraged bear with an arrow lodged deep in its muscled shoulder. Someone failed to kill it and the poor animal could do nothing but rage and remain in denial of its imminent demise. The Brute clambers to his feet, remarkably unscathed. He nods appreciation to The Driver, she smiles kindly and retrieves her blade.

Atop the mound of rocks, the deer is gone. Only sunlight in its place. A pity, but The Brute is strangely pleased. He is glad the deer will never be stuffed full of straw by a lousy taxidermist. The bear on the other hand … He looks at the corpse, the steam rising from the still-warm fur, and grins. The Driver notices his reaction, frowns and asks nonchalantly:

"Any chance we can eat it?"

"At this point, I'd eat right about anythin', and a bear ain't lookin' too bad."

THE FIRE CACKLES AS THE meat sizzles amid the flames. The weary travellers huddle around the meal; they are vultures perching atop stones and fallen tree trunks. Their faces sunken with defeat, minds lost within dreams of better days. The Brute watches each in turn. He knows no names, only faces. He measures their usefulness.

First, the two men: The Mandolin, a stout man with thinning hair and a second-skin of sweat, brings a smile to The Brute's face and is currently peacefully tuning the strings of his instrument. And The Slaughterman, gaunt with jet black hair but barely old enough to form stubble above his lip. He skins and cooks efficiently, but there's a prickly nervousness to the way he prods and jabs at the bear.

Now, the women: The Fugitive has cagey eyes and sealed lips; she was found coming from the South into The Brute's hometown on horseback with her wrists shackled and a bullet in her leg. Then there's The Farmer, curly straw-blonde hair and eyes the gloomy grey of a rainy day. She's stocky, with toned arms from shovelling and digging; her husband died a long time ago. Finally, The Maid, still young and sweet but lonelier than all the rest combined. She lost everything when her home burned down. At night, he can hear her sobbing under the old oak tree.

They all sit in silence, safe for now in the eye of an unpredictable storm. The Slaughterman slices off a slab of bear meat and chews it. He seems satisfied and motions for the rest of the travellers to dig in. The Brute removes his knife and gets himself a chunk large enough to fill him up. Juice spills from the pores of the bear meat, making him salivate. He retreats to the shadows of the stone wall to eat in peace.

In the night sky, an eerie white fog wraps around a strip of stars. The crescent moon peers at The Brute with a judgemental glare. Its ghostly white light bathes down on the neighbouring terrain, illuminating the shrubs and trees and stretching their shadows out toward his dark hiding place. Yellow light flashes in the eyes of hungry animals as their irises are reflected in the heavenly body's stolen luminosity.

A forest stretches toward the looming backdrop of a snow-capped mountain, where wolves howl to proclaim their dominion. The leaves are lightly dusted in snow, making them slightly less ominous than usual. A circle has formed within the forest, where the trees can't seem to grow. In this circle, there's a Girl With Hair Like A Storm. She's standing in a fern field and has her head tilted toward the moon, as though its light can breathe a new soul into her reanimated corpse.

The Brute watches her with wariness but continues to eat his dinner by the solace of his stone wall.

A METALLIC STENCH STINGS HIS nostrils. The sky is a thick, heavy veil cloaking the face of God; but its once smooth silkiness is now creased and sagging, threatening to crush the world. God grows weary in his high tower, reminiscing on the mistakes of his creation. A storm is coming.

The Brute wonders why he thinks so often of religion, his mother was never a devout believer, and yet it is all that fills his mind of late. Perhaps the nearness of death is a door to enlightenment.

He presses the butt of the rifle into his shoulder and feels it jerk satisfyingly into his muscles as he pulls the trigger. The clap of gunfire, then the bullet splinters through a tree. Dead-centre. Birds scatter into the sky and The Brute slides another round into the top of the rifle. Barely aiming, he shoots down a bird. It releases a final squawk before plummeting from the sky.

The young man, The Slaughterman, is standing next to The Brute and watches all of this with a keen fascination. He snatches the gun from The Brute and slaps the ink hair from his ocean eyes. His lips retract, exposing teeth like jagged rocks. He calmly prepares the firearm for more mindless butchery, though the quivering of his hands betray his honourable doubts.

The rifle is worthless without a bullet lodged within its chambers and a ruthless man to pull its stiff trigger. It contains no prejudice or motive but is still burdened with the blame. A tool to cleanse the endless yearning, an instrument of death that requires the skills of a musician. The question remains, how do you silence an orchestra?

The Slaughterman holds the rifle incorrectly at his hips like a shotgun. He eyeballs a tree and dangles the barrel toward it, with a loose grip and looser finger.

The rifle shudders, vomiting lethal bile, and then there's a spark of yellow light as the fired bullet ricochets off a stone. The smooth slab is chipped, the lead has left a scar. The weapon, frightened by its own power, leaps out of The Slaughterman's hands and flees for the open sky. His hands are sliced open in the process, two red slits smiling with devilish glee, the palms of an impulsive man.

The anger comes to a boiling point, The Brute can see it in The Slaughterman's veins. "You did this!" The Slaughterman squeals, "cause of you we had to leave. Now I gotta shoot this gun, I gotta eat bear and sleep in a damn tent. I dunno what I'm doin' or where we're goin', I'm scared they'll find us. And all of it is 'cause of you. All of it!"

The boy leaps at him, trying to find something of sustenance to grip or to punch but managing only to snag the loosely-buttoned shirt. The Brute does not budge. He's a head taller than The Slaughterman and looms over him with contained fury. The Slaughterman, like a leech, hangs from the thin cotton shirt as though there's an empty grave below.

The leech whimpers, and The Brute's soft green eyes glaze over with a coating of cold steel, losing all compassion. The grave beckons them both.

"Then leave. I ain't askin' you to stick around." He grips the leech by the back of the neck, twists and pulls – as you're supposed to do with these kinds of parasites – and throws The Slaughterman to the ground.

In the sky overhead, The Brute sees a dark and false lighthouse. Its silhouette lost beneath a moonless sea. He blinks away the infectious imagination. He knows what's real. What's real is the empty grave that's now luring with siren songs of lost love.

The Slaughterman and The Brute are separate. One crawls in the dirt, scalded by his tears, the other waits and watches with bloody handprints on his clean white shirt. The grave opens wider with grinning teeth and winking eyes.

"I can't leave. I got nowhere to go." The Slaughterman screeches, "but they're comin' back. You know it, I know it. They're gonna find us. The Faceless Strangers don't leave no one alive. That's why they call 'em that, they skin ya alive! They skin ya alive." He kneels in front of The Brute, head bowed and hands on knees to steady himself. The boy sobs. "They're gonna bring their guns and their horses and it'll be real messy and real bloody and right now, it's lookin' like we're all probably gonna die."

"You ain't gonna die. Besides, what do you expect me to do about it? I did what I could the last time those Faceless Strangers came knockin'." The Brute defends himself.

"You did the best you could? Where were you the day they came? Where were you when they hurt ma? When she was alone and scared on the ground and they – and they – I was unconscious, I had tried to stop them and –" The Slaughterman breaks down, "I want to go home. I just want to go home and see my ma again. I don't want none o' this, I don't wanna shoot nobody. She was gonna make me eel pie that night, my favourite food and she was gonna make it. I never said – I barely saw her that day –" The Slaughterman kneels there, crying.

The Brute doesn't know what to say. He waits patiently and tries to remain detached. He doesn't comfort the boy but instead tries to convince himself that it's not his fault, that it is a sad thing that happened but that he can't blame himself. He wishes The Slaughterman would quit crying. It's beginning to get on his nerves.

Eventually, the boy stands up with a blank look in his eyes and walks off somewhere. The Brute sighs with relief and looks at the ground that The Slaughterman has left behind. The grave is still there.

He decides he needs more sleep. He's used to being in cemeteries, there's always work to be done there and he's never one to turn down a quick buck. But he has never seen a vacant grave as he does now. One that materialised out of nothingness with a mean glare and an emptiness to it. He is losing his already lost mind, there's only grass here. There's only grass. He's being foolish, hallucinating a six-foot deep hole in the middle of a forest. What was he thinking? There's no such thing as an empty grave.

***

SUN-BLEACHED ROCKS HIDE BENEATH FROTHY waves. Seagulls nibble away at the remains of a broken man. He's been impaled on a jagged rock and already barnacles cling to his soggy skin. Seaweed ties him down, shackling the twisted remains. A lighthouse peaks over the horizon, its light swings around and around and scours the seas. But the corpse is just out of the light's reach.

***

THE MAID IS SURPRISINGLY ADEPT at horse riding. Feet inside the stirrups, she applies just the right pressure to dictate the direction and desired speed of the horse. The mount trots alongside The

Brute's stallion and willingly responds to the girl without a fuss. It has taken a liking to her.

It was her idea to go riding. She'd woken him at the early hours of dawn and led him over to the horses. She couldn't fit the saddle onto the horse herself, if she had been capable, The Brute is sure she would've ridden off by herself without bothering to wake him. Nonetheless, he attached the saddles and accompanied her, and now they're riding through the thick forest as the sun climbs further along its path to the dark side of the world.

The Maid admires everything in sight, childlike wonder thankfully not lost amidst all the grief. She reaches out and touches leaves or tree trunks, pressing her hand against the rough wood. The Brute longs to feel the same things, to look in awe at the world around him, as he did as a child. Those days are long past.

She has not spoken to him since they began their journey. She enjoys the silence as much as him. The Brute appreciates her willingness to simply ride, letting the day gradually pass while they ignore the threat of doom that lurks in the cellar of every waking thought and conversation.

She's skinny. Too skinny. He can see bone pushing against the inside skin of her forearms, and her Victorian blouse hangs loosely from her shoulders. She's in a blue prairie skirt. The Brute had recommended trousers, for more maneuverability on the horse, but she'd refused. Her hair, barely scraping her shoulder, hangs choppy and straight. But it's her eyes that upset him; the wide oval marbles no longer sparkle, there's an absence, a hollow space where something used to be, a ghost of a shape. That's all that's left. They keep riding.

At a stream, they break for water. The shallow wash of waves over pebbles soothes The Brute and the horses; they feel calm. Safe. The Maid is a ways off, she looks over and smiles at him and The

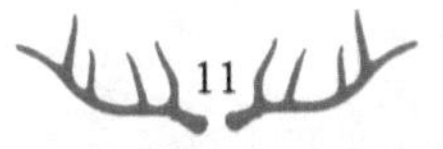

Brute returns the favour. She removes her satchel and unscrews her flask. While bending over to fill it up, something comes into view behind her. A Girl With Hair Like A Storm. Facing away from The Brute, toward the mountain.

***

THERE'S BLOOD DRIPPING FROM HER fingers. He can still hear the droplets, the constant dripping against the wood. Her body strewn out across the floor like a trophy. Or a warning. Her eyes rolled back into the tops of her head, searching for heaven and seeing only black. The Brute's there but he turns away now and walks out the door, trying to remain calm. Trying not to think. There's snow everywhere and it's cold and it's winter. Tracks lead away from the house, already disappearing beneath fresh powder. The Brute goes back inside.

THEY RIDE ALL THROUGH MIDDAY in silence. At some point, they make camp and The Brute falls asleep. When he awakens, it's dusk. The girl has prepared a fire and caught a rabbit using only her knife. She's cooking it on a spit. She smiles when she sees him and he finds himself smiling back. Unusual.

"We need to head back. The others'll be worried." He says. She frowns and glances at the foreboding trees.

"Not now, in the mornin'," she replies, and though the obvious assumption would be she's afraid to ride in the dark, The Brute knows there is a far grimmer reason. The night is her time to weep and remember. She cannot live during the night when they do not. He understands the comfort in the quiet of night, the solitude. He simply nods, returns to sleep and lets her grieve.

MORNING COMES AND THEY STUMBLE across a camp. Empty, though there's still smoke rising from the ashen fireplace. The shape of horse hooves in the sludgy mud reveal the camper to have left recently. Very recently. There's a burlap sack tucked under a tree. The Brute moves over to inspect.

"We should go," The Maid says, but The Brute shakes his head and unties the thin coil of rope wrapped around the tip of the sack. He peers inside; apples mainly, though some other fruits and vegetables are muddled in as well. There's also a fresh pair of trousers and a shirt, some shoes too. The Brute closes the sack and flings it over his shoulder. He heads back to his stallion.

"You can't take that!" The Maid yells.

"What's it look like I'm doin'?"

"Whoever that belongs to, you've killed him."

"One less person to worry about."

"Please, leave it. We got plenty food," The Maid pleads desperately. The Brute looks at her over his shoulder, her desperation. He nearly agrees, nearly turns around and places the sack right back where he found it because he knows she's right. But then he looks at her again, those skinny arms, the shading around her sunken eyes, and the paleness of her skin. He can't let her stay like this, even if she hates him for it.

He straps the burlap sack onto his saddle and climbs atop his horse.

They ride in silence, but this is not the comfortable silence from before. They've issued a death sentence to a stranger who, to the best of their knowledge, has done no wrong. The Brute can't make this right with the girl, he knows this, but every so often he attempts to make eye contact. He needs to know she still acknowledges his existence.

Has he failed her by keeping her safe? Will she resent him forever, or will she come to understand? He doesn't care about the man they plundered. His camp was deserted. His belongings were discarded. A steal waiting to happen. They were merely responsible for the inevitable. If an action is predestined, surely The Brute cannot be held accountable, and The Maid will have to forgive him. He feels guilty, without a doubt. He once brought the grim reaper to her doorstep – to everything she holds dear – but he also truly cares about her.

"I don't wanna see you become a bad man," she says, startling The Brute.

"I've been a bad man for a long time now," he replies. She ponders on this, looking north to hide her face from his.

"Says who?"

"Me."

"Suppose no one would know better than you," she says with a shrug. He smiles at that.

"Maybe not. I'm just a man holdin' a gun, tryin' to run from a murderous gang who wants to kill 'im. I ain't got nothin' under my hat but hair," he responds, finally. "You know, you're clever for your age. I wish I had a daughter like you," he says this absently, something kind to say to a promising young lady.

The girl drops her head and grips the reins tighter. Her horse quickens its pace so that she is slightly ahead. He tries to read her, the straight posture and tenseness of her muscles. Finally, she says without turning around:

"If I were your daughter … would you let me die as she did?"

And The Brute's blood runs cold. He doesn't know how she knows, but he hopes she's the only one who does. And if she is, he hopes she can keep a secret.

***

A MEMORY. A DREAM?

He's a boy, perhaps six years old, riding in the back of a wagon with his mother. She's alive. Her eyes are clear orange. Her hair's straight and brushed. There are no bags under her eyes or blemishes on her cheeks. She's humming, reading a book. The Brute hates reading but loves stories, and he hopes she'll retell the book's tale later in the evening in her unique way. As she always used to do.

Riding shotgun is a man who may be the boy's father. A slick ponytail and a clean-shaven, prominent jawline are the only distinct features. The rest of his complexion is a blur of mismatched parts. One eye? Two? Green, possibly? A gold tooth? Next to the man riding shotgun is the stagecoach whip, directing the hulk of wood along a dirt road. Both are wearing goggles to protect their eyes from the swirling dust cloud caused by the hundred or so wagons ahead of them.

They're in a large group, a typical way of migrating from one place to another, but the boy only knows his mother. He's frightened by all the commotion, the loudness of the horse hooves and the way the dirt itches his skin. The dust cloud presses against the wagon, creaking the wood and making it bend inwards. It's his mother who keeps him from panicking; she cracks some joke about how the men resemble ugly bugs and tells him he'll one day be somebody who matters.

He hates the journey, but at least she's there. At least she'll always be there.

***

HIS HANDS ARE TREMBLING.

The Brute is holding a large glass vial that reeks of burnt ichor. He's an adult again, and the memory – which had felt so real, like he was reliving that singular point in time – vanished in the internal dust cloud.

Now, for some reason, he is standing on bright red grass in a foreign forest. Green vines curl around the trees, pulsing with crispy energy. Huge leaves curl around him like furry wool coats, he reaches out and touches one of them and the leaf pricks his finger. The black sky spectates overhead and mocks his human stupidity. The beast above is withholding and cavernous. An empty womb, an empty tomb. There's hardly a difference.

Somewhere ahead, a rumbling voice is talking loudly and The Brute can hear a kettle whistling. He tries to walk and finds that he is actually floating a few inches above the ground. The Brute begins to glide through the forest at a great speed. Birds wait silently in high-trees, they have no eyes and their beaks are sewn closed. They do not fly or even move, but their presence is nonetheless unnerving.

The Brute passes a dying deer. He can hear its lungs deflating with a drawn-out wheeze. Its stiff mouth dribbles blood and it moves with jerky twitches as it tries to force itself to its feet. However, instead of antlers, the deer has snakes protruding from its forehead. The Brute continues to glide past the dying creature and ignores the other strange animals in this foreign place.

He enters a clearing where The Mandolin and The Farmer are sitting at a long table covered in an assortment of platters, such as raw meat in the shape of cakes. There's a willow tree guarding over this unusual engagement and to the left is a caravan that has candles atop its roof. The candles have green flames and if one were to peer closely, they'd find: A ghostly man clasping both cheeks in the midst of a scream.

The Farmer clambers to her feet and lumbers over to the screeching kettle. She pours four cups of tea and carries them over to the table, placing them at various empty seats.

Two spirits flicker into life, gouging on the uncooked food and sipping gingerly at their tea. There's a man in a bronze crown who's hunched over in his chair like a scavenger scouring the ground for lost coins. He has a pistol strapped to his side and bead bracelets around his bony wrists. Next to him is a being with an owl's head and a snow leopard body. She purrs as she sips from her china tea cup.

The Mandolin notices The Brute and gives him a crooked smile: "Hello?" He says. The Mandolin is in a pearly white dress coat and can't seem to stop fidgeting with his bowtie. "I apologise, but I'm afraid we ain't got no more than four teacups. You're still welcome to join us, sir. Have a seat, let's talk." He motions at a vacant chair, The Brute – through no will of his own – finds himself sitting down.

"Let's hear what he thinks on the matter." The owl says, her voice mimicking a whistle. The spirit swallows a wriggling worm whole.

"I don't think he got no opinions." The Farmer says.

"That's exactly what we need." The old hunched-back man croaks. He gazes at The Brute with grey eyes and a wrinkled face that looks like a sun-dried peach. "Whether he's a brute or a man; he has fresh eyes and a working mouth. So, what do you think, Brute?" The old man has a lightning streaked beard which he now scratches vigorously as a dog with fleas would.

"Who are you people?" The Brute asks, calmly. Nothing about this feels out of the ordinary and he does not question the reality of what surrounds him.

"I am the anointed one, The Slaughterer of Man. That there," The old man points at the owl-leopard hybrid, "is The Caretaker of this place. She owns the land and we are her guests. Now, with introductions out of the way, tell us your opinion."

"My opinion on what?" The Brute asks. And suddenly, everyone at the table freezes. It's as if time has stopped and they are perfect marble statues capturing the final moments of their supper.

In silence, the company stares blankly at their teacups. The

Mandolin and Farmer are leaning away from each other, trapped in a position that creates a V-shape with their bodies. Their faces resemble the Mona Lisa – expressionless – but behind the gaslit oils are hollowed-out eyes that leak deep secrets. Then, after a minute, they move again.

The Mandolin's bald head gleams with sweat. He pushes away his teacup and picks up a violin from under the table and begins to play The Bach Chaconne in D Minor. The Farmer stands up and carries a shovel over to the darker patches beneath the willow tree. She begins to dig.

The Caretaker pounces to her feet and prances over to the caravan. She opens the oval-metal door and the hinges squeak triumphantly. The Brute glimpses the inside: A mountain of treasures, discarded and forgotten. The door closes but not before The Caretaker grabs something in her beak. She comes back to the table and tosses it onto the mahogany wood. It's a painting.

The Brute tries to make sense of the illustration. There's a wooden raft on rough seas, a cyan-coloured wave is rolling toward the vessel. Piled on top are sailors, some are naked and half-drowned others are clambering over each other to try and peer over the crest of the wave and glimpse the great beyond. The mast leans West and the sails are stretched tight in the wind.

"It's a painting." The Brute states his initial thought on the bleak artwork. He removes his leather, ten-gallon hat and places it on the table. From his waistcoat, The Brute unpockets a tobacco leaf and his harmonica and begins to chew one and play the other. He loosens the handkerchief around his neck and rests one of his spur boots on his knee.

"It's The Raft of the Medusa!" The Anointed One explains as he picks up a gold coin from the ground.

"It's grim, is what it is. Only a lunatic would have painted that."

"Do you think the men will be saved?" The Anointed One asks.

"Mammon!" The Caretaker screeches.

"That is not my name!" The old man growls in return, "Besides, I am simply asking a question."

"I don't know," The Brute says. "I don't think it's none of my business."

"That's a double negative," the owl hoots. As she says this The Mandolin finishes playing violin and The Farmer returns from digging. She tosses her shovel into the woods and places the severed head of The Girl With Hair Like A Storm onto an empty platter. The others begin to eat, digging into the girl's eyes and ripping off her tongue with their forks.

The Brute swats the head off the table and leaps at The Mandolin, grabbing the musician's head and slamming it into the table until the flat nose bursts open and the dark wood cracks. Grabbing his ten-gallon hat and tossing it into the face of The Anointed One, The Brute unholsters the greybeard's gun and blows the old man's brains out. There's a splatter and a thud, then the other's die:

The Farmer drops dead without a second thought. The Mandolin's head explodes and brain matter sprays everywhere like pieces of mouldy sponge. The Caretaker's internal organs seem to come alive, her intestines leap out of her mouth like worms that wrap around her neck. She suffocates and dies. Their corpses boil and blister and within seconds, they're screaming puddles.

The Brute doesn't understand what just happened. There had been no emotion attached to his violence and now he still feels empty. The head of The Girl With Hair Like A Storm is face-down in the dirt. Discarded.

A hooded figure arrives on a stagecoach. The four horses huff and sniff and bellow hot steam into the air. The figure removes her concealment and reveals herself to be The Driver, scratched and bloody from claw marks. She motions him aboard and they race off into the deeper parts of the forests. At some point, they totter on the edge of a cliff. In the distance, riding the waves, a quiet lighthouse beckons.

The paint is peeling from the spire's walls, exposing stale orange bricks. The rocks holding the watcher in place are insecure, loose. Then, as The Driver continues to lead the stagecoach further away, The Brute watches the lighthouse collapse and sink beneath the waves. Lost forever.

They emerge from the forest and enter into a sunlit meadow. There's a cabin in the distance and the horses gallop with great speed toward the open door. The Brute steps out of the stagecoach – leaving behind its gold plated door handles and red, velvet padded walls. Immediately, The Driver vanishes into thin air.

The Brute enters the dingy cabin and ignores the ash-covered deer head on the wall and the enticing smell of a meal being cooked – it smells like his mother's cooking but The Brute pays no attention to this fact.

He focuses on the young lady sitting at the dining table. Her cheeks are a soft red, her shoulders are slim but slightly toned from a life of fighting and running and her dress is long and elegant but with a simple cotton design. The Maid looks over at him, but she doesn't smile–

***

THE BRUTE AWAKENS FROM HIS dreams. He's lying in the dirt by the old stone wall. The moss is wet and slick against his back. Over by the main campsite, the others are crowded around a burnt-out campfire, sleeping fitfully. What disturbed him from his slumber? Already the memories of childhood and the strange world of spirits and cabins is departing from his mind.

The Fugitive is a few feet away, watching him. She's silhouetted in the expired light and quivers with indecisiveness. Her grey hair hangs in her eyes and almond skin is plagued by goosebumps.

He shifts to a sitting position and unbuttons his damp shirt, tossing it to one side and putting on his vest. The fugitive steps closer and the expression on her face – a shattered ceramic cup – makes The Brute wish he could remember his dreams. Perhaps he talked in his sleep; exposed himself in some way.

"I need your help," she forces, arteries popping at the side of her neck as if an unseen spirit is squeezing the words out of the half-empty flask of her body. "Please."

The Brute reluctantly replies, "with what?"

A CHOIR OF TREES SURROUNDS them; the ground at their feet is lilacs. A blue lunar bulb is swinging from the ceiling of the night's sky. Its shine refracts against the flowers, blurring the pink into something reminiscent of northern lights that shimmer like crashing waves. A thin stream of water runs past them, fireflies flickering above it. They're in a wonderland.

"What is it you want from me, then?" The Brute asks her.

"I need to climb that mountain." She points at the snow-capped mountains that backdrop the forest. "Before those people come back and kill us."

"Why?"

"Wherever we go when we die, I don't think I'll see my husband there. I need to say goodbye. The mountain is where I must go to do that."

"Why the mountain? Why not here? And why do you need me?"

"You'll see the power of the mountain when we get there. As for why you; you're a killer, a brute. Who better for protection?" She tells him, smiling. The Brute considers her proposition. The

journey would take days, they may struggle for food, and for what? To talk to a dead man.

"No."

Her face falls like an avalanche but it doesn't faze him. He starts to walk away.

"I don't blame you for what happened," she calls out, suddenly, making him stop. "They all do, but not me. They think it's your fault and they may be nice when you're around, but when you've got your back turned they spit and growl and talk about all the ways they hope you die."

"Well, maybe they're right and you're wrong," The Brute says.

"They are right, it is your fault. There's no getting around that. You brought those savages to their homes. I don't know why they came, what you did to provoke them into burning the village and massacring the people, but you brought them."

"But you don't blame me for all that? Because you need me?"

"I don't blame you because I forgive you."

"Please," The Brute scoffs, "That's the same as pretendin' it didn't happen."

"No, it's the same as acknowledging that you're not the centre of all this. The tragedy isn't your own personal sin. It's a grief that belongs to all of us. I forgive you because what else is there to do?"

"I done nothin' to warrant forgiveness."

"You're still here. Aren't you?" The Fugitive's voice is passive but there's a hiss to it that's overtly dominant.

"So?"

"I seen worse things in my life than you. But if you want me to stay on your side, you need to help me. Come to the mountain with me. Otherwise, when the shooting starts, and believe me it will, you'll be the only one they aim at. So, what do you say?" The Fugitive extends an open palm toward him. The Brute considers her offer.

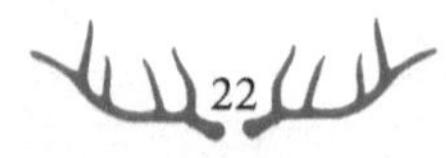

In the distance, wolves begin to howl.

THEY LEAVE AT DAYBREAK. THE rest of the travelling company see them off from the other side of the stone wall. The Driver offers to accompany The Brute, and though he could use an extra rifle, he declines. The others would starve without The Driver's hunting skills.

He says farewell to The Mandolin and The Farmer but his heart isn't in it. There's a sourness hanging in the air that The Brute can't pin down. Both of the travellers have a casual gait and a posture that is so neutral it screams bizarre. The Slaughterman at least carries his spiteful hatred with honest dignity, but The Mandolin and Farmer are Russian babushka dolls.

Even The Maid brings a pang of pain. He regrets, more than anything else, his choice to steal the burlap sack. She has good reason to hate him, more than anyone else because she is so young, so innocent, and until recently she had seemed willing to give him another chance.

She had no reaction when learning of The Brute's choice to leave, and now she doesn't even look his way or wave goodbye. Instead, she stands under the willow tree. A scarecrow propped up to scare him away.

He ponders on the book of Genesis. Who was worse? The serpent offering tainted apples; or the unforgiving God who banished his greatest creations from the utopian garden, stole their immortality, and forced them to live in this place. This premature hell. Was the serpent ever truly evil? Was it not free will that birthed darkness in all mankind?

The Brute and The Fugitive head toward the forest on horseback. Above the mountain, dark clouds are at war amongst themselves. A battle cry of thunder, followed by the slash of lightning, then the foggy grey is torn up into rain. The mountain shows no disturbance.

RIDE, HUNT, SLEEP, CONTINUE. THIS is their routine.

For nine days, they sit on a saddle and clatter onwards but the mountain never grows larger. It remains the furthest object in sight and continues to shrink away from them. On the ninth day, The Brute discovers he can discern the outline of a cave in the centre of the great chunk of rock and he takes this as a sign to talk to his companion.

"Where you from?" He asks her.

"I grew up in Taxco de Alarcón, it's this scorching, deep south town. You won't have heard of it, not many lived there."

"What was it like?" The Brute continues questioning in his gruff voice. The Fugitive is silent for a moment, smiling at something The Brute can't see.

"I remember there was this chapel I used to visit, The Santa Prisca Church. It was made from this beautiful pink stone and there were two towers on either side with bells at the top. Inside, the roof was a colourful tiled dome and there were golden altarpieces that stretched all the way to the ceiling. I used to say prayers and when I left I could see out across the crimson roofs and behind the town was the mountain and I felt safe. I felt so safe." The Fugitive's voice falters and her horse slows. The Brute slows with her.

"Why did you leave?" The Brute queries softly.

She shrugs. "I first met my husband in Mexico City. We learnt English and a few other languages together. When he died I came here. On the way I shot fourteen men and stabbed a fifteenth."

"Do you regret it?"

"No."

***

Naked skeletons washing in a river: The Fugitive gives herself some distance and faces away from The Brute, but he can still make out the thick white lines scrawled across her olive back. Deep and unhealed.

They have arrived at the great mountain. They tie their horses to a tree, very loosely so that the animals can wander around and survive off grass. Then they prepare for the final stage of the journey.

The mountain's pregnant belly hangs over them. Snow runs down its face like melted makeup and jagged cracks smother its plump body in unwanted acne. They are at its feet, where unnaturally long toes dig into soft earth. Does the mountain fear it will float away unless it anchors itself to the dirt? The Brute bites back his dismay.

The earth-bound entity is disappointing. From a distance, its size and power seemed sacred. Its contours and edges were smooth, and its white-capped peak was a diamond breaking through the boundaries of Nirvana. He can't see the spiral tip now, the crest is hidden from sight. He had thought the mountain was a seat built for God himself. The Brute never considered why it might have remained empty.

Now, standing at its base, he acknowledges that the journey was fruitless, for him at least. There is no enlightenment, penance or forgiveness here. The stone is just stone. The snow is just snow. And the mountain will eventually be eroded by the same gusts of wind that first built it. Like all things of past, present and future, the mountain is no more permanent than man. And the cycle will always return to the place it began; nothingness.

The climb is hard and steep. His alpenstock – a staff with a pointed blade at the end – keeps him sturdy, but the elements pull no shortage in punches. Icy glass slices into his eyes and hissing ghosts try to throw him off the cliff face. However, if insignificant little mountain goats can do it, so can he.

The path slants at an almost vertical angle. He can either lean into the storm, charging toward the peak like a bull, or roll down to the bottom.

Behind him, The Fugitive flickers in and out of view as the snow flaps around her like a pale curtain. Her lantern eyes glow from a gap in her cloak and tufts of dark hair stick out, trying to run from the freezing cold. He waves at her. She waves back. A sign of life to show that neither has died. They continue upward. Toward the stars shimmering beneath a peeling blue sky.

WOLVES. OF COURSE THERE ARE wolves.

He can hear them under the quieting storm. At the summit, they howl, waiting for a much-needed meal. He can picture their matted and grey fur. A pendulum of drool swinging back and forth, hypnotising you into climbing into their warm jaws. Then cosiness. Not felt for a long time. And finally, that feeling of sharpened teeth slipping into your numb skin, the sweet release of built-up blood clots clearing out of clogged veins and the smell of vindication.

THEY CAMP IN A CAVE and huddle together for warmth. A tiny fire – closer to being a lit matchstick – burns in front of them but The Brute can't feel its heat. He's never known cold like this. Outside, the dying words of foreign folk are whisked through the air. Unrecognisable wailing. The amount of it suggests a massacre has occurred somewhere in far off lands. Why is the wind only ever the carrier of bad news? The Brute needs to hear some good news.

The Fugitive snuggles into him. Her eyelids are closed and she takes deep steady breaths, but he does not think she's sleeping.

Now and then a shudder runs through her like a pulse of energy, electrifying her heart and keeping him awake.

The cave is an indentation in the mountain, a half-formed globe. The walls are smooth, damp and cramped. On the ceiling is a myriad of crude drawings done in red and black. Figures. Animals. Places. All mingling together in the dancing firelight to create a moving picture that tells a thousand stories, none of which The Brute can decipher.

An army of snow marches into the cave and guns down their fireplace, murdering it in cold blood. The freeze sets in and his bones clink and jangle, trying to spark some warmth into his rubber body. Like some ghastly horror from an old gothic tale, The Brute crawls and heaves his way over to the white caked wood.

Kneeling over the remains, he gets to work rebuilding. The Fugitive stirs and mumbles but stays sleeping. He blows onto the embers and red ash billows into his face. The Brute coughs but keeps blowing and, with a reluctant sigh, the orange twigs sputter to life.

He can feel his muscles loosen and soon he can move his fingers again. Once the fire is well and truly up and running again, he crawls back over to The Fugitive, wraps his arms around her, and falls asleep.

MUSHROOMS. SHE WANTS HIM TO eat blue-spotty mushrooms.

They've nearly reached the top. A long journey is coming to an end. The final stretch is a sloped river of frost shrouded in fog. They have not started wading through yet. Right now, they are on a patch of grass, where the mushrooms grow. The Brute does not know why The Fugitive has stopped. He observes her as she drops to her knees, removes the knife from her backpack and cuts each fungus at the stem until she has a pile of fungi in front of her. Then she tells him:

"We will eat these," and motions at the poisonous, squishy delectables. He knows nothing about the mushrooms. He assumes that they are native to the mountain, having never seen them before, and wonders how The Fugitive learned of them. The thought of eating one fills him with dread.

"Why?" He asks, keeping his tone relaxed.

"They will unlock your mind to acceptance. They only grow in high places," she tells him. "We will go to the very peak of this great rock and open our eyes and look."

He does not know if that was meant to inform or bewilder but nonetheless he takes a few of the mushrooms in hand and, with nothing left to lose, flicks them into his mouth …

Sourness. Snake venom trickling down his throat. The mushrooms bubble away in his stomach acids. Sizzling. Spotty-blue everywhere. Can't see. The world stretches, wraps around itself again and again like a never-ending spiral staircase. The shattered pieces of a mirror float in front of him. No reflection. Only a Girl With Hair Like A Storm, trapped on the other side.

The Brute turns around and vomits. His head clears slightly and he realises there's a whirring train engine everywhere. He can't shut it out. The headache is piercing every fabric of his person and body. He faints.

"I DID NOT MEAN YOU should eat them immediately." The Fugitive kneels over The Brute with an ice-cold damp cloth. He sits up and rubs his head. "If you eat them here, the visions are horrifying. Only on top of the mountain can you safely consume the mushrooms." She explains this like it's obvious. The Brute wishes he knew all that before eating the horror-inducing fungi.

He staggers to his feet, shakes himself off and starts for the hill. He wants to finish this quest and be done with it.

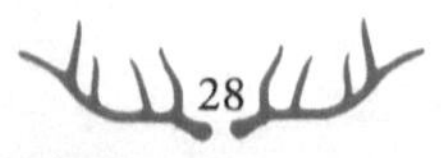

He loses sight of The Fugitive quickly. She disappears behind puffs of velvet cloud and when he calls out to her, the only response is an echo. All he can do is keep going and hope she's not far behind – easier said than done: There are no landmarks, only the frost and the fog. The Brute could walk straight off the edge and not realise what was happening until he was plunging straight into the depths of hell.

The fog smells similar to the mushrooms and The Brute worries what that might mean. His leather boots are already damp inside and sharp frost shards chew on his leg. The river-like path is waist-deep, he's slowly losing control over his body as the cold spasms become more frequent. His face is permanently frozen in a snarl and his eyes burn and water simultaneously. Needless to say, he's not going to last much longer.

A figure passes in front of him, or a shadow. It floats smoothly across the landscape, a black splotch of ink on white canvas. It has no arms or legs and its head is a thousand faces grotesquely mashed together. Strips of cloth trail behind the being and tied to the ribbon-like material are enslaved people. They're smaller than The Brute – possibly dwarves? – and hobble with stumped legs, shuddering in the naked light.

He knows what he sees can't be real, but being trapped in the tangle of ribbons for eternity seems a fate worse than death. He pities the dwarves. No wonder there are no true fairy tales. Anything magical or fantastic would be hunted or enslaved long before any brave hero would save them.

The Brute pushes onward, letting the figure and its slaves disappear behind him. He passes more strange creatures along the way, all hidden in mist. Some have too many arms or legs, others are plain smooth spheres flying or rolling down the hill. None pay him any mind.

At some point, he stumbles over a skeleton covered in gold necklaces. Its rib cage is crushed bone fragments. The eye sockets see everything, and the jaw moves wordlessly, trying to share centuries of lost wisdom. Its bony hand cracks as it reaches out to grab him. The Brute keeps on moving.

All the things he sees move down the hill, as if running away from whatever's at the top. The higher up, the thinner the mist, and objects begin to take on proper shape. Ahead, there is the silhouette of a leafless tree – resembling a crooked old man leaning over the brink, deciding whether to jump – and a cave where shapes move in the shadows.

The Brute has made it. He's so close. He looks behind and spots the outline of The Fugitive. She's not dead! Perhaps their luck is beginning to turn. He turns back towards the cave and sees them emerging: Wolves. At least half a dozen. Exactly as he pictured them that first night in the mountains. He had hoped then the howling was far off. Now, they dart out of their hiding place.

And suddenly, it's night. The sun leaves them. Without word or warning, it throws them into the dark innards of some dead creature. The snow blindly searches for them, but the wolves know precisely where they are. They come toward The Brute slowly, taking their sweet time.

The Fugitive arrives next to him, fearless. How she found him so quickly is a miracle. She unhooks her backpack and removes two wooden sticks from inside (the tops of them are wrapped in cloth) and a matchstick box. She quickly begins lighting the sticks. Has she done this before?

He catches one of the torches and holds it in front of himself; the smoke stings his eyes and a flash of burning houses skewers through his vision. He blinks clear and notices the wolves have now encircled them. The Fugitive presses her back to his and they spin slowly, trying to keep an eye on each of the six wolves.

The torch hisses and coils. A guiding light, a ward for evil spirits, but not something the wolves fear greatly. Its orange snarl bounces off the boulders and turns the white snow into molten gold.

The wolves toe the line where the light reaches, stepping into the heat for a second before retreating into the comfortable grey. He can't see them fully in the darkness. All he notices are glaring bulbs, the eyes of predators, watching him. He spins around and around like an overworked clock, he is the hour hand and she is the minute. The wolves' glowing eyes blur as The Brute spins faster, until they are streaks of yellow stretching to create a wall, entrapping him.

The Brute waves his torch like a lunatic, knowing it will do nothing to impede the approaching wolves. The beasts bark and snarl. Their tongues – a stirring spoon to mix their saliva into pots of bubbling froth – whip loosely in droll mouths.

The Fugitive splashes something in the soft snow and, when The Brute arrives at her side of the circle, he notices she's leaving a trail of dark liquid as she twirls. Before The Brute can ask what she's planning, The Fugitive drops her torch in the snow and a ring of fire erupts around them. Blocking them from the wolves and searing the hair on The Brute's arm. The inferno is as tall as The Brute. The rest of the world has vanished.

Immediately, tar-like people clamber out of snowy graves to wash clean in the flames. The melted goo of their skin runs down slimy bodies in droplets that pool at their feet and feed the fire. They dance, hold hands, hug or stand perfectly still. They move their bodies in every possible direction, except the direction that will let them leave their ring of fire.

Men, women, children, even babies all crawl and writhe in

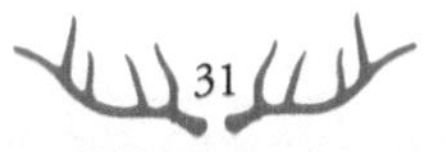

the blaze. Faces sheets of wet black, masking agonising screams. Webbed fingers snatching at tufts of fire. They are punishing themselves; The Brute doesn't care why. All The Brute listens for is the continuing crackle of greedy flames, and the receding whimper of wolves. He hears the beasts fleeing into the coldness of their caves. And he grins.

HE CAN SEE EVERYTHING FROM up here. A sea of stars, each a perfect diamond, watching over every rolling hill or troop of ants. The shadows blend it all together and for the first time, The Brute realises that it's all the same. One. Connected. Whole.

There are differences between each rock or strand of grass, but in the end, they are still just another intricate part of the land. Serving their purpose. Then moving on. Without repercussions. That's the happiest thought The Brute has ever had in his entire life.

The Fugitive lights an oil lamp and holds it out over the edge of the cliff like a warden guarding the mountain pass. Where she was storing an oil lamp this entire time is a question The Brute will never be able to answer. She removes a few mushroom heads from her pocket and eats them. She holds out more mushrooms for The Brute. He takes them from her and swallows them whole. The acid is stronger this time. He gags and holds in bile. Then, The Fugitive hands him another already lit oil lamp, which he holds as well.

"Thank you. For coming. The wolves are new, most of these places are empty – save the spirits, course. Times are changing." She tells him. "The first time I climbed one of these was with my husband. His sister died. I didn't see anyone. I hope you don't either." Then she kneels in the snow, places the oil lamp at her feet and begins to pray. A halo of light forms around her.

A rumbling starts beneath The Brute's feet and dust sprays against him, he is reminded of waves crashing against a stony beach in the dead of night and the loneliness of such sounds. The valley rises to meet them. The river below stretches out toward the horizon and the trees loom tall, old giants wishing farewell. The mountain is sinking! Actually, sinking suggests a slow descent, this is more of a plummet.

Soon, the dirt is all The Brute can see. Pink worms, roots and brown cake that's wet with fresh rain. The sky above is reduced to a shrinking hole where the mountain once was. Only one star is visible now and it's dimming the further they sink. Darkness encases them. This rock is their tomb. The only light is the oil lamps: Bubbles of holy yellow. Why is The Fugitive still praying? Whispering words like gunfire, eyes peacefully remaining closed.

***

RED. ALL HE SEES IS red.

The cabin is covered in it. The girl is dead. The supplies are there, waiting to be taken. The Brute's racing heart finally slows. He looks at the corpse with empty sockets.

***

THE BRUTE STUMBLES AS THE mountain crashes to a stop. The earth has opened up to a cavern. He can sense things here with him. Forgotten fossils at the centre of the earth. He glances toward The Fugitive and notices she's no longer kneeling. Instead, she hovers in midair, shining her oil lamp on the face of a man. His hair is slick black, his skin oily olive. They talk in whispers The Brute cannot hear, but he admires them still.

The Fugitive swings her oil lamp toward The Brute – as if to introduce him to her late husband – but as she does, the yellow washes over a pile of moving bodies: Limbs detached, bones protruding, skin peeling. Her oil lamp continues to swing onto The Brute and the bodies vanish in darkness. The Fugitive says something, then returns her attention to her husband.

The Brute collects his oil lamp and inches forward. Exploring. The cavern is large and his light is too small to illuminate much. The first thing that enters his golden globe is splayed fingers with overgrown fingernails. Next, arms and legs like spiderwebs entangled together. Eventually, the whole grotesque fiend enters The Brute's private sphere. It pumps with a beating heart and a thousand blood-stitched eyes that pierce his soul.

"Do you remember me?"

The Girl's sweet words of innocence. The Brute turns around then puts his back up against the monstrous corpse collection. He stares at the speaker; The Girl With Hair Like A Storm, and shivers. The Brute takes comfort in the warmth of the dead carcasses.

"Yes. I remember," he says and she nods.

"Thought maybe you didn't. Do you still think about me?"

"Always." There's tears in The Brute's eyes.

"Why?"

"I try not to but you're still there, in the cabin."

"You left me there."

"I know."

"Why didn't you bury me?"

"I couldn't. I should've."

"Did I do something wrong?" Her eyes are moons, pale and lifeless and empty but The Brute can still hear the pain in her voice. The whimpering. He's sobbing now, and his body feels torn up and out of place. A snapped matchstick.

"No," he forces out. "You didn't do nothin' wrong."

"And now I never will," she says solemnly, all the sweetness gone. And then she returns to the darkness that she came from and The Brute is alone with the beating heart of a fiend.

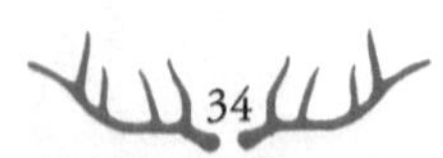

Two days ago they journeyed down the mountain. It was easy. No wolves or spirits or storms. The rest of the ride, so far, has been equally easy, but long. They're still riding now; his feet are swollen and blistered and his back is in agony. He didn't ask The Fugitive what she saw that night nor she him. Each had their own private epiphany.

However, there is something he wants to tell her – needs to tell her – and nowhere seems better than here; in this jungle of leaves, vines and soggy mud. So, he looks at The Fugitive with her graying hair and slumped shoulders (he notices for the first time how short she is), then he takes a deep breath. He empties his mind and says:

"I killed a girl. That's why those people, that Faceless Strangers gang, came and raided our town." It feels both good and sickening to hear it out loud. Finally owning up to such a hideous crime and receiving the forgiveness or punishment he deserves. The Fugitive doesn't look at him. His words barely register.

Is she tired? Or just doesn't care? The Brute continues, "I had been huntin' but there wasn't no game around. It was winter, and I seen a campfire just North. They're camped in an abandoned town. Tents everywhere but main cabin had lights on so I went there. Thought it'd make a good lootin'.

"They had supplies, a lot of supplies. And I swear to you there was no one there, I mean, I thought there was no one there. She came out of nowhere and I fired. It happened so fast. It was a gut-shot, she bled out slowly I think. Shoulda stopped and seen to her but I didn't. She screamed and screamed and crawled around like a damn banshee.

"My horse had this small cart attached and I stocked it full of them supplies, quick as I could. Left the little girl there on the floor like she was nothin'. Blood was everywhere, up to my knees even. For someone so tiny she had a lot in her. Only took about a half of their loot before the men started comin'. Then I left, and they followed and I think they're still followin'. Their campsite will be movin' the same way as us for better weather. They lost winter provisions, doubtless the warmer Southern lands'll be perfect to regain them. The Slaughterman was right. They'll be here. Sooner or later."

The Fugitive still doesn't reply and The Brute drops his head in shame. They continue their journey back to the rest of the travelling group.

STILL NO RESPONSE FROM THE FUGITIVE. They're camped and eating cooked rabbit. The meat is chewy, but the wetness helps and The Brute is hungrier than when he first ate that bear. How long ago was that? Winter when they first arrived, and now late summer. It can't have been that long.

Out of a bush, mama rabbit appears, ears flat against the head and pupils so dilated the rest of the eye vanishes. Her white fur is coated in mud and her paw is bleeding. He can't imagine what she had to go through to get here. She watches solemnly from the edge of the campfire as The Brute and Fugitive feast viciously on her children.

"MY NAME IS MARIA. I think you should know that, before I die," The Fugitive says to The Brute after another night of ignoring him. The Brute's breath catches in his throat. What should he say? Why would she say that? He panics and stops his horse in its tracks. She looks back in confusion and The Brute composes himself and summons all his willpower.

"I'm Colt," he says and Maria nods. He thinks that was the right thing to say. Maria's brow arches as fragments of golden light crack and slice through the green canopy above them. Colt dismounts and leans against the rough bark of a tree, trying to remain relaxed. A brown spider blends in with the tree and rests there with him.

"Colt? Odd … I heard that name meant; Home Protector. You're certainly living up to your reputation." She seems on the edge of laughter. Colt's face flushes. He runs his tongue over his teeth, tasting the piano keys connected to his gums.

"No. My mother told me it meant; from the dark town."

"That's a strange thing to call a child. Besides, your town isn't dark, it's only ash," Maria continues without him and then Colt is once again The Brute without a name and Maria is a faceless fugitive and it is like the conversation never happened. He begins to ride again, following closely behind The Fugitive, and forgets what he didn't hear.

The Faceless Strangers have arrived.

The dreaded gang has provided a welcoming gift. A mutilated horse. The legs are torn backward and the exposed bones are chipped from dog bites. The Farmer is already dead. She's turned over on her side, staring at The Brute with pale white snow-globes. Soaking red intestines stretch from her open stomach like tree roots.

"She was tryin' to run," The Brute says.

"Survive," The Fugitive corrects him.

"Ain't no fair. Prolly didn't even put up much of a fight."

"You don't know that."

"Yeah. We should say a few words," The Brute says and they dismount their horses and quickly tie them up at a tree. He removes his hat, "I'm— I'm sorry. This wasn't your fault … I never even knew your name, but I am sorry. I hope that— Well, I hope there's something better and wherever you are … I hope you're grinnin' wider than a baked possum." The Brute chuckles and wipes his eye.

"You ain't very good at this, are you?" The Fugitive says. To the West, a scream shakes the air and startles the birds. The Brute and Fugitive unlatch their rifles and crouch in the tall grass.

As they move forward, the ground vanishes and becomes waist-deep muddy water. They walk slowly, so as not to disturb the water. Their rifles remain pressed to their shoulders. The leaves dip low, shielding them from the blood-red sun.

The Farmer's body – a frozen statue, encased in snow – slashes through his mind. It doesn't matter if she hated him. He spent so long convincing himself that no one blamed him that he forgot what it would mean if they did. It meant nothing. How they felt about him was irrelevant because he would never acknowledge their thoughts. He is a coward.

The Farmer is gone now because he brought these people here, good people turned bad from grief. So much death and so much violence and he is the cause of it all. A Brute who butchers little girls.

He subsides a sob and catches the rustic scent of burnt bark. The forest is on fire. Red tongues lick green skin. Already, the stone wall has crumbled like bread, the moss has melted, and the willow tree curls and burns.

From somewhere out of sight: The crunching of The Mandolin's delicate instrument and the snap of each string breaking under the weight of some tone-deaf frontiersman's boot. The Brute winces and imagines The Mandolin lying warm on cold ground. The balloon of his gut sliced delicately open in a perfect slit. His entrails steaming, raw and red.

They slosh quickly through thick water, trying to find the broken instrument. Gunfire strikes and the tall grass strands are sliced in half. The Brute dives headfirst into brown, dirty sludge and becomes entangled in the submerged roots and branches. He twists, turns and pulls but the water keeps him in its grip until, eventually, hands drag him upward and then he's coughing up weeds and mud.

The Fugitive crouches over him, cradling his head. They're hidden on a patch of land with thick undergrowth. The Fugitive's eyes are cat orange, a blend of warm honey and grey filth.

The Brute thinks of his mother. How she used to bathe him, her fingers entangled in his hair as she hummed fairytales of wolves finding lost and broken toys and bringing them back to children. Or demons who cursed the moon and stole it from its rightful owners. His mother's orange eyes were always glittering.

Why does he remember her now? Is it the blackened trees and dead bodies? The desire to return to childhood? Back when he was still the sweet boy in the bath? It doesn't matter. It's too late now. He is the demon from the story and he has stolen the moon. There is no one to stop him. In a just world, that boy in the bath would've drowned so that The Girl With Hair Like A Storm could've lived. But this is not a just world. And both of them are dead.

With The Fugitive's help, he stands up on the uneven ground and wipes the mud from his face. He lost his rifle somewhere but it doesn't matter. None of it matters. He's going to set things right, no one else will pay. The Fugitive waits for him to say something.

"Let's go find the others," he tells her and sets off to find friends, and hopefully a gun.

THEY FIND THE MANDOLIN AND Slaughterman flat on their stomachs beneath the wagon. The large man is lying in a pile of his own vomit, his face is wet and soggy from crying. The Slaughterman, on the other hand, hisses when the pair come too close. "You did this," he howls, "you did this. It's your fault that they're here."

"I know," The Brute says calmly, "but I'm gonna make 'em leave. You're gonna be alright."

"Am I?"

"Trust me."

"How are you gonna make 'em leave?"

"I'll kill 'em."

"No you won't. But you can let 'em kill you. It's you they're angry at. Whatever you stole from 'em. They want vengeance."

"And what if I let that happen and they kill you anyways?"

"Then they're bad people and you're not culpable."

"I still led 'em here," The Brute convinces. "I can't let none of you die. But maybe you'll get your wish and one of 'em'll land a lucky shot," he says, cracking a smile and rubbing his unshaved chin.

Ironically, a shot thunders in The Brute's ears and the corner of the wagon explodes in splinters. He dives to the ground and takes refuge under the wagon, with the other two. The Fugitive crouches and scans their surroundings.

"There!" The Fugitive hisses. A few yards away, a pebble is disturbed by an unruly elbow. The tiny stone was resting atop a triangular mound of rocks but now rolls from its throne and onto the dirt below. The Fugitive's hawklike vision shifts and she points upward at the source. The iron gun barrel is exposed by a pebble, it glints angrily.

The Brute crawls and then rolls to his feet. The Fugitive gives him a sideways stare and they set off. Their movements one and the same, they glide toward the lone gunman, skimming through thick undergrowth and skeletal trees. The Brute relishes the sweet countryside; it's warmth and visibility. No snow to hide horrors, no mist to stick against his skin like clothes of ice. Only a dripping red sun and smudged clouds and a lone gunman.

The pair dive into the ground at the base of the mound of rocks. The Fugitive clutches her rifle tightly and nods at him, "I take him out. You take his gun." She tells him, already moving off before he has the chance to nod in agreement.

The Brute is about to follow when, to his left, he glimpses at least half a dozen frontiersmen rising out of the nearby murky swamp water. Tattered seaweed hangs from the green moss of their skin. They're a trained firing squad who aim their rifles at the wagon, where The Mandolin and Slaughterman are camped, and without hesitation fire six bullets directly into the duo's skulls.

"No!" The Brute bellows. The Slaughterman's head pops like a watermelon, splattering everything in the nearby radius with the thick pulpy pink of his brain. The bullets that hit The Mandolin seem to sink deep into him with a squelch, as if his head is a wet, mouldy sponge.

"You bastards!" The Brute growls and the firing squad take notice of him. He hears another gunshot above him and hopes The Fugitive has killed her enemy. He turns regretfully away from The Mandolin and Slaughterman's bodies and climbs the mound of rocks to retrieve another gun from another corpse with another pound of vengeance weighing on his mind.

The Brute takes a steady breath.

There is something intimate about someone placing you in the sights of their rifle, to stare down the deep hole of the barrel and know the bullet that lies in there will be the end of you. It's humbling to understand that the man with his finger on the trigger is prepared to take your life.

The Brute and The Fugitive are in a standoff with the firing squad, who are now situated behind and inside the wagon. The Faceless Strangers Gang move in frenzied blurs, the sun backlighting their figures. Taking all of them out at once is impossible and revealing their position would be suicide, so The Brute and Fugitive wait. For an opportunity, or an escape route.

THE OPPORTUNITY EVENTUALLY COMES IN the form of an explosive cart. It rolls down a high hill and must have been stolen from wherever The Faceless Strangers are camped. The cart crashes into the wagon where the marksmen are situated and erupts in a fireball of heat. By some bizarre miracle, four of the men survive the blast and scramble to their feet, prepared to fight.

From the same hill, The Driver and The Maid – like heroic cowboys – gallop downward on two mares, with their hair tied back and faces glistening from the heat. Pursuing them is about a dozen footmen, and one horseback rider, screaming and shouting wildly as they blast their rifles every which way with little accuracy or care for who or what they hit.

The Brute watches all this with fascination. Meanwhile, The Fugitive is leaping to her feet and charging valiantly toward the remaining marksmen. She aims down her rifle, taking down two men with swift shots.

The Maid spills from her horse and crashes onto the dirt. Her slender body is scooped up by a Faceless man, and a knife is pressed against her throat.

Fear fills The Brute. The kind that consumes you and dissolves your thoughts in coal-fueled incinerators. His pearl skull is stained with soot. His wide-brimmed hat is the anchor-point that keeps the vertigo at bay. He galumphs down the mound of rocks, scraping his shins and tearing his clothes.

Fire and snow blur each eye: His home burning. His feet frozen. His people's pleas for help. The Girl's wordless corpse. The stuffed deer head melting on the wall. A crowd of pitchforks singing church songs. The screaming siren for daughters lost. The stench of death. And the constant pursuit of Faceless Strangers in endless storms.

The Brute reaches The Maid and tackles her attacker. A fury of punching, scratching, biting and downright catfighting ensues. Moral codes or masculine-approved styles of fighting are forgotten with both The Brute and his assailant resorting to whatever means necessary to survive another year of cold, warmth and life in the wild west.

The Brute hears, more than feels, the popping of his own eyeball as the attacker slips a talon under The Brute's eyelid and tickles the inside of his head. Memories scratch away like stamps peeled off an envelope, dates and people blurring into obscurity. The red is everywhere. His. The assailant's. The Girl With Hair Like A Storm. His mother hanging by her neck from the barn ceiling, blood trapped in her head like an overstuffed scarecrow. Red, everywhere.

The Brute lashes out blindly, finding a grip on lightning locks that seem vaguely familiar. The Brute opens his good eye and catches a clear glimpse of his opponent. A square nose pressed against a flat square face with square ears poking out either side of his head like soup bowls. But it's the sight of the man's wiry hair that cuts off The Brute's steady stream of adrenaline. The Brute jerks away from the hair that reminds him so alarmingly of a black ocean on a stormy night, and he finds The Girl With Hair Like A Storm lost in the emeralds of her father's eyes.

"No. No, no, no, no, no ... it's you." The Brute releases the man from his grip and raises his hands in surrender. He takes a slow step back before the man removes a small blade from his boot and plunges it into The Brute's belly. The wound startles more than hurts him and The Brute collapses backward. The girl's father wraps his hands around The Brute's throat.

"You're 'im, aren't you? You're the one that went an' took 'er from me." The man growls and squeezes tighter, "Look at me. Look at me! Ma' name is Daniel Sunday, I lead this 'ere gang, we're the Faceless Strangers. Ring a bell, son? You stole from us. You took ma' girl from me. Now, you're gonna look at ma' face and you're gonna know that this is what you get. This is what you get you sonofabitch!" Foamy saliva sprays from Daniel's mouth, cleaning The Brute's wounded eye.

"Please. I'm sorry." The Brute can barely choke out the words. He struggles limply to pry Daniel's hands from around his crushed windpipe.

"Sorry? I lost everythin'."

"—was an accident. I didn't mean—" The Brute's eyes roll back in his head. There are no stars in the afterlife, only a black sky. Everything that matters is behind him, the past is set in stone and a legacy is all that survives. Only at death's door can one finally understand this, that is life's way of getting the last laugh before throwing you from its thrashing back.

Regrets pour through him; burning his body like fiery gasoline. Where was his father? Why did he leave so long ago? What did he look like? Where are The Brute's kids? Why don't they exist? And finally, what was the point of it all? All the murdering, lying and running only for him to end up strangled by some gang member with no one left alive to bury his body afterwards.

Suddenly, the hands quit squeezing and pine-scented air eases into his lungs. His eyes slip out of the thin darkness back into bleary sunlight and green forests. The Maid has leapt onto Daniel's back, her teeth clamp down onto his ear with the ferocity of a ravenous dog. Her hair whips around her and those sweet eyes are bloodshot fireworks. Her cracked lips scrape against Daniel's skin and her pale body is a silkworm writhing around his body. The Brute meanwhile is paralyzed, his brain is still sleeping.

The Maid throws her head back, ripping a chunk of meat with her. Daniel howls and slaps a hand over the exposed bone. He charges backwards, slamming The Maid into a nearby tree, her head knocks into the trunk riddling her unconscious. Daniel kneels on her chest and grabs a nearby rock, raising it high into the air and preparing to bring it down onto The Maid while The Brute helplessly watches helplessly from the ground.

Leaping off a horse she stole from the Faceless Strangers, The Fugitive swoops in to save them. She blasts her rifle, sending a bullet straight through Daniel's back. She then throws a dagger into the man's skull. He growls, unaffected by the blade protruding from his head, and curls around with the complexion of a one-antler Wendigo spirit.

Now some sort of possessed entity, Daniel bounds toward The Fugitive and drags her to the ground. The grieving father twists and pulls at the knife in his head until it comes free – along with goo and bone marrow – then he offers The Brute a vengeful smirk before slitting The Fugitive's helpless throat.

The Brute wiggles the pocketknife out of his abdomen and tosses it away. He crawls toward Daniel and The Fugitive, digging nails into dirt. His face is droopy, his muscles don't respond properly and he's leaving behind a trail of blood like a snail.

The world tilts upside down, The Brute is hanging onto the earth with all his strength, gravity is tearing open his wounds. He loses his grip, falls.

***

HE'S STILL FALLING. DEEPER AND deeper into a gradually shrinking hole. Rows of ghastly candles shimmer and stretch. His fingers crumble away, sand particles floating back to the surface. Is this death? There was no warning, no life flashing before his eyes. No anything. One minute he's crawling and now he's falling. No, he's not dead. Not yet. This is something different. It has to be.

The hole shifts. He's whole again and rising up through the ground and into a meadow.

The Girl With Hair Like A Storm takes her tiny hand in his wrinkled one. Purple cornflowers grow in a circle around him, spheres of prickly petals. White feverfews grow around the Girl, soft and gentle. The flowers seem to sprout up beneath their feet as they walk together in silence. It's so quiet. So peaceful and cloudless. All The Brute can hear is the gentle rush of water from the distant waterfall that marks the edge of the illusion. An edge looking out over what, exactly? The Brute doesn't know.

They head toward a cabin. A pile of logs, rectangular in shape, with two windows and a door in the centre. A cat's perched sullenly on the tiled roof, tail sweeping back and forth with slow precision. Inside, the dining table is set with a porcelain teapot, herbal tea, and three plates of sheep sorrel pie. On the kitchen bench is a bowl of calf's foot jelly, The Brute's favourite dessert. His mother is singing softly to herself as she puts the finishing touches on her gourmet dish. With a jolt, she notices The Brute and Girl.

"Oh, you're early!" She hums, taking off her apron. "Come, sit. I made it just how you like it." She leads them to the table, still singing a song under her breath. She seats The Brute and Girl side by side at the table then scurries gracefully back into the kitchen. The Girl examines the mother, then passes The Brute a wary look and squeezes his hand tighter.

"Mother—" The Brute begins.

"Hush now, children! Your father'll be home soon."

"My father?" The Brute says, even uttering the words seems foreign.

"Yes. And be kind, he's back from the war."

"What war?" The Brute asks as his mother finally sits herself at the table. Her posture is straight and rigid but there's a relaxed calmness in her orange eyes and a serenity to the summer dress she dons. Behind her, in the window, the cat purrs while the moon rises. How did night fall so quickly?

"She's a quiet one," his mother says, speaking of the Girl quivering in her seat. "Hello darlin', I'm Abigail. What's your name?" Abigail leans forward, craning her neck to smile over the frightened Girl. The Girl says nothing. "You know it's not polite to ignore your elders." Abigail scolds then begins idly gazing at the grandfather clock at the far wall, losing all concentration.

"Mother?" The Brute asks, Abigail's eyes remain fixed elsewhere. "Where are we?"

"Home," she replies.

The clock chimes and with it comes a knock at the door. Glowing life leaps into Abigail's body. She rises promptly and glides to the door, unlocking the numerous bolts and locks that posed no problem for The Brute when he first entered the cabin, mere moments ago. The door swings open and in steps a shadow that never settles into a shape but rather flits between outfits and body sizes with the messiness of a toddler's drawing.

The shadow noiselessly seats itself at the table, Abigail joins them. The Brute glances down and finds his plate stocked full of food, it tastes of dirt and dissolves in his mouth. The Girl doesn't touch her meal, she keeps her head bowed and avoids eye contact, continuing to grip The Brute's hand fiercely. The shadow hefts up something from within a coat, he drops it on the table. Alarmingly, The Brute realises it's a dead cat, the windowsill is empty and dark. No moon. No feline.

Abigail prods the furry carcass, muttering, "Such parasites. Lurkin' out there, huntin' …" She sits back and stares at The Brute and

Girl, sizing them up. Abigail's lips move incessantly as she chews on her inner cheeks. The shadow stands and tumbles over to the fireplace with all the subtlety of a boulder. He stands there, patiently. Abigail ignores her husband's movements.

The Brute struggles to speak. Despite being aware of the bizarreness of the situation, some part of the whole affair seems perfectly natural. Every action occurring, every word spoken, is all a preordained moment that passes in time and then ceases to exist. There's no history here, they're in a clock that ticks forward then resets in a constant cycle. Anything can happen here and nothing happens at all. But why? What brought him to this place with such strange people?

"Is this real?" He asks, knowing the answer but believing it to be the only sensible question in a pool of irrationality.

"No," Abigail says. "Not to you."

"Am I dead?"

"No."

"You really her then?" The Brute squeaks, his heart thumps.

Abigail smiles sadly, rubs her neck. "I don't know. I suppose, maybe."

"Why'd you do it?" The Brute's fighting back tears, "I loved you. We were happy."

"Son …" Abigail pleads.

The Brute doesn't relent: "I missed yer funeral. I couldn't see yer face again, or that grave. It didn't seem real. From the moment I found you hangin' there everything else was gone. All the happy times lost and all I could see was yer cold corpse swingin' from that barn ceiling and no reason for it. Why didn't you gimme a reason, ma? Why'd you just up and leave? You spent so much time whinin' about my father and you go and pull somethin' worse, at least he was fast rippin' off the bandage, I had no reason to miss him. I

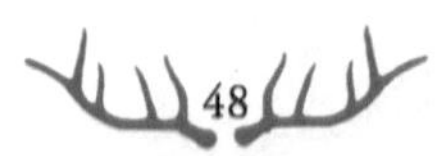

missed you, ma. Everyday of my life I struggled, so imagine my surprise in findin' out you've been here all this time, cookin' and singin' to your heart's content like you done no wrong."

"This ain't proper dinner conversation, son. Wouldn't you rather enjoy your meal?" Abigail is fragile like a porcelain doll. She keeps rubbing her neck until a mean rash forms on the suddenly pale white skin.

The Brute tosses his fork onto the table. "Proper dinner conversation? No, you don't get that. I've spent a lifetime hatin' myself and hatin' you. I dreamt so often of bein' face to face with you again, one last time. I'd sit down calmly and say, 'look at me. Look at what you did. What you created.' And then it'd all be out in the open and I'd leave you there, to wallow in your guilt, and move forward."

"I ain't takin' the blame for who you are."

"Oh yes you are."

"Fine. If that's how you want it then say it and be done with it."

The Brute ignores her, "Y'know, those first couple' years, after you passed, I spent some time alone walkin' from town to town, servin' booze in saloons and stealin' from folk who didn't give no shit about me. In all that time I ain't found a reason, just ways to keep forgettin' over and over. Joined gangs, fought for money, stole from the better off. Killed so many folk. Good folk, bad folk. Don't matter no more. I done some … awful things. You coulda stopped it.

"You said I was special, I meant somethin'. I want you to look me in the eyes and tell me that was jackshit. You sit there with a fuckin' dead cat and a fuckin' shadow and you don't acknowledge shit. Tell me, ma. Tell me what it all meant? Tell me why you did it? Why'd you break me, ma? Why'm I broken? Tell me!" The Brute's standing up, his fist smashes down on the table, he's half-pulled the Girl out of her seat. He calms his breathing and sits down.

Abigail sighs. "How come you went and killed the girl, son? Who could do a thing like that?" she asks, catching The Brute off guard. An electric current passes down his arm and The Girl With Hair Like A Storm lets go of his hand, as if only now realising who he is. Where she knew him from.

"What?" The Brute queries, slowly and with great care.

"Did she have a reason to die? What was the meaning behind it?"

"It was a mistake."

"You think her daddy told her stories about the moon like I did? Made her think she was a princess who'd grow up to live in a castle with the handsome prince? It's all horseshit, boy. I never loved you because I liked you. I never wanted to sit up late each night bathing the mud from your knees. I had to do that. Make you feel safe. It's what a mother does.

"I did what I did for me. It ain't got nothin' to do with you. Son, you're actin' like all these things that happen, somehow you're the centre of it all. I'm here to tell you that you ain't shit and all this … it ain't shit neither. Everyone dies, who cares who's fault it is or what it all means. Life don't have answers, it don't even have a rudder. Who you are ain't gonna fix that. Sure, you done some bad things and you deserve to die, but don't you dare act like I'm the cause of it all, or that my love is the saving grace that's gonna bring you salvation. If you think that, then your knife's so dull it wouldn't cut through hot butter."

"No. That ain't true."

"How much did you really know about me? What'd I do for a living? A whore, a barmaid? Is there anyone left who can tell you? This sweet child might have meant somethin'. She sure was im-portant to that Daniel Sunday. But me? You and I? This is it. This cabin is everything. You remember when I first took you huntin'?

You shot that deer poorly and it ran off for hours, bled out before we found it. Suffered and died without dignity. We butchered the meat and put the head on our wall because it made you feel proud. I told you you did good. But I never took you out huntin' again."

"What's that to do with this?"

"What's anythin' to do with this? You're havin' dinner with two dead people and a figment of your imagination because that's the better alternative to a life of damnation. A life of tryin' and failin' to do right and matter and understand. In the end it's futile. The small things count to you and the big things count for the world."

"That don't make no sense."

"Makes more sense than life."

"You're telling me right and wrong don't matter. Your death, the girl's death, That don't matter?"

"We're all graves by the end, only some graves are dug deeper than others." Abigail solemnly states this, then rises and gathers the empty dishes for the return trip to the kitchen.

The Brute wants to say more, but he can't think. There's a buzzing in his ears, the Girl keeps tugging on his arm and mouthing something but he can't discern what she's trying to tell him. Eventually, his attention is drawn back to the shadowy figure looming over the fireplace. Something strange is taking place.

At first, The Brute thinks his vision is playing tricks on him, but then the smell of smoke reaches him and he knows it's real. Half of the shadow's form is leaking into the fireplace and igniting it. The fire solidifies the thing's body, oil drips from his stiffened limbs, and he is consumed by flames. Within moments, The Brute's 'so-called father' is reduced to a pile of molten goo and the fire is tracing its way through the maze of floorboards.

The Brute calls for his mother in a panic only to see she's hung herself from the kitchen ceiling. The flies hovering nearby and the decayed green flesh peeling from bird-chipped bones suggest she's been there a good while.

The windows to the cabin flap open and a cold winter gale sends snow billowing in, barring the exits. The cat, alive and well, purrs curiously on the table. Its black coat peppered with frost.

The Brute snaps himself out of his shock and realises the Girl is still tugging relentlessly on his arm. He glares down at her, balancing on the thin edge between anger and fear. The Girl is clutching a bullethole-stricken stomach. Her shirt's been stained with a giant rose, the hole at it's centre pumps gallons of blood, blooming the flower across her torso. She opens her mouth and a waterfall of gore pours out. Stabilizing his own breathing, The Brute wraps his arms around the Girl to stop her violent shivering while the cabin crashes down around them.

Red embers float like fireflies, the wood cackles gleefully. The roof caves in and a thick beam smashes through the floor. The fire licks at his skin but doesn't burn. The Girl similarly remains untouched by the fire, left to soak in her blood and die slowly. Wordlessly. On the far wall, the stuffed deer head quivers and blinks, its beady eyes staring fearfully into the flames. Trapped in its place on that wall. It lets out a hoarse scream that's equally raspy and high-pitched.

The Brute cries and stares at The Girl With Hair Like A Storm. So small and innocent. His fault. His mistakes. He doesn't deserve it, to have been born into a good world with good people only to make that world worse and leave those people dead. Why him? What went wrong in that process of creation? Did God forget about him? Went to take a long piss and a nap and forgot about poor old Colt?

And then he's falling and the cabin, the Girl, his mother and the fire are all above him. He can see through the floor up to the

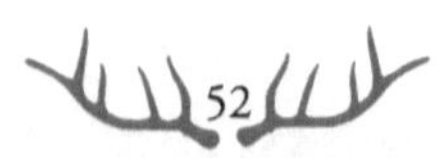

ceiling. As he falls he watches the Girl run from the cabin, a stream of light pours from the open door into the darkening smoke. Then the door shuts, the cabin burns and The Brute falls eternally.

***

SUDDENLY HE'S BACK TO CRAWLING toward The Fugitive as though no time at all has passed. Daniel shifts in and out of focus, giving the impression of several changing photographs: At first, Daniel's still kneeling on The Fugitive's chest. Then, black. Now, he's standing over The Brute. Black. The whites of Daniel's shark like teeth against the stark red ichor smothering his skin. Black. He turns his back on The Brute. Black. He's hobbling to a tree. Black. Daniel collapses in the shade; his storm-like hair quits cackling, all it is now is rotten straw. Black.

The Brute doesn't care about Daniel's lack of final words. The absence of closure. He doesn't care that there was no forgiveness or penance, that The Brute didn't have to pay for his sins and that Daniel didn't deserve to die. He ignores the implications that he was the cause of all this, the catalyst for a massacre. All he cares about is crawling forward and focusing his eyes on The Fugitive. Just reach her.

He snatches The Fugitive's hand. Holds it in his own. Their eyes lock, her life refracts through those dilated pupils, unwieldy and random: Her husband, bloody and crying; a train ride nearly stopped by bandits; people kneeled and shot in hot desert sand; The Fugitive on horseback whispering to herself over and over "My name is Maria. You're from Taxco de Alarcón. Stay alive. Stay sane."

Her life is out of order, disconnected moments sewn together with thin string, tug a little hard and it will rip at the seams. She smiles at The Brute now, those memories baptising her, cleansing her. Washing gently through her mind until she slowly fades away.

The pain from her wounds is a dull ache. She lived a life of breath-taking experiences and true love, that's more than most can say.

The Brute imagines her in a cave filled with colourful malachite crystals. She's swimming in a lake. Her husband is there. They kiss and make love and at night those crystals glow green and paint the cave and its translucent waters. The heart of mother nature.

The serene wishful thinking ceases when The Fugitive grabs a fistful of The Brute's shirt and releases a guttural cry that sprays her entrails into the air, a most violent blowhole. In that final moment she's reminiscent of a wild billy goat. There's nothing human left of her. It's sad to realise that everyone's final seconds reduce them to a primal beast desperate to do anything for one last dawn. It almost makes the rest of their life seem inadequate. Wasted, even—

"Maria," The Brute pleads. "Maria, you're gonna be alright. You're gonna be just fine, Maria. Maria? Please, be alright. Please. Maria?" He shakes her warm body, and cries.

The Farmer is dead. Then The Mandolin and The Slaughterman. Now, The Fugitive. Please Lord, let that be it. Let there be no more.

The Driver patches him up as quickly as she can. There are still Faceless Strangers lurking and doubtless their camp isn't far, meaning a second wave could still be on its way. The Brute finds himself on horseback, with The Maid and Driver riding alongside. The Driver holds a rifle in one hand and horse reins in the other. Someone must have attacked her because she is covered in claw marks that bleed profusely.

They gallop through towering trees with thin trunks and bristling leaves. As the sun dips lower and stormy grey covers clear blue, a thin mist leaks across the forest. How quick the world went from high humidity to a cold, desolate dreariness. For such dense woodland, The Brute feels incredibly alone.

The edges of the horizon are tinged purple and those last traces of light are slowly being eaten away by the black hole of darkness. Soon, the heavens will be consumed by night. The stars come later, only once the dark has won and the light has ceased do they dare shine bright. The Brute continues to flee toward the last sliver of purple, investigating his surroundings as he does. To the North, rolling hills and growing mountains. To the West, a straight plane of desert where nothing grows. The South lies behind them, a warm cemetery.

It's midnight when they hear them.

The Brute and his companions have long since slowed their progress and now travel at a canter. Tendrils of fog wrap like coils around The Brute's legs, threatening to pull him down into that frightening place between life and death where all bad deeds and purgatory folk lie waiting to torment him.

At first, he thinks it's merely their own horses making that rap-tap-tapping against the cold hard ground. But it's not. It's them. Who else could it be? And then The Brute and his companions are fleeing once again, in what is now beginning to feel like an endless cycle of running and dying then running some more.

How many Faceless Strangers are there? Surely such a large number of people aren't devoted to killing The Brute and his companions? After all, he only killed one girl and stole a portion of their supplies, and for it they burnt his town and killed anyone ever affiliated with him. Is he missing something? Their revenge, while warranted, is undoubtedly petty.

The pursuers are catching up to them. They must be riding at the speed of a bullet. Within seconds The Brute will be overrun. He glances at The Maid, she's ghostlike – an aura of honey yellow radiates from her skin, a beacon guiding them through the shadowy patches. The Driver is a block of moving marble, every kick of her heels into her horse's side is deliberate and with purpose. Together they ride, but the gap between The Brute and his pursuers is gradually narrowing.

And then, five mysterious horsemen gallop past. Apparitions which shimmer a hazy blue. They pass through The Brute like a rush of cold air and leave a well of sadness in their wake. Immeasurable sadness. He remembers his mother waving goodbye to him before he went off to the local store, the last time he saw her. What she looked like: The pale blue eyes and the mouldy dark patches, a disease of tiredness. Her hair frizzy and her bones pushing against her thin skin. She was so frail. And that smile. Lopsided and half-formed like she couldn't quite remember what it was she was supposed to be trying to smile about. Then she was gone.

Looking over, The Brute glimpses similar memories passing over his companions' faces. None of them say a word, instead slowing their pace and trying to gain control over their emotions.

He is thankful whatever was chasing them wasn't the Faceless Strangers, but he wishes those bizarre demons hadn't left their pain and misery swelling inside of him. Although, perhaps it's better to be in constant pain and to suffer than to be empty. That is The Brute's greatest fear, to wake up one day as cold as those he's killed but still able to breathe. What then?

So peculiar this past year or so has been, The Brute doesn't even question the supernatural nature of what just occurred, a spirit of some sort entered his body and imprinted part of itself inside of him and that seems normal. Instead of pondering, he accepts it for what it is; another brief instance of enlightenment in the American frontier.

***

As they edge deeper into the forest, the mist slithers into their mouths and noses. The place is peaceful for the most part, the demon riders are in far off winds. A quartet of ghosts carried swiftly off to haunt the next poor soul.

The Driver leaves them at the peak of twilight. "I was a bank robber. Used to run with folk like these and trust me; they don't give up easy." That's all she says. No heartfelt goodbye or a promise to one day meet again. One second she's there. The next she's gone. And The Brute and maid keep riding.

The Maid doesn't leave him. He doesn't know why she chooses to stay but he's glad. When they ride past several bodies hanging from a tree, their faces peeled off, The Maid makes no mention of it. However, she later stifles a scream when they ride past a deer being consumed by maggots; its shape still visible beneath the swarm. They continue riding.

Eventually the trees thin out, the mist clears and both agree it is time to rest. Whatever tomorrow brings, at least no one can say that they didn't fight for their survival. As a cloud fades away and vanishes; so too his hometown, everything it stood for, is forgotten.

***

Days pass and the journey into the unknown continues. Some day soon they will reach a wooden bridge, the planks and ropes swaying back and forth rhythmically. The bridge will lead to a lighthouse which The Brute will climb. Atop the lighthouse will be a beacon. The beacon will shine its light onto the ocean. In the ocean, in its depths, The Brute will see; the scattered remains of friends, and the smiling faces of enemies.

***

He flicks the match, hunching over it to prevent the howling wind from snuffing it out. Shaky fingers transport the tiny flame into the remnants of a dead campfire and blacken the crispy wood. Once the fire is up and going The Brute seats himself away from the harsh heat and enjoys the warmth.

The Maid is opposite from him, her form flickering and distorting like a mirage that will disappear should The Brute squint too closely. She is pale and her cheekbones push against her skin. There's a medallion swinging from her neck, one he has never noticed before. It's too dark to make out the details but it's crescent in shape. They're in a cocoon of shrubbery yet somehow the wind still manages to creep in on them and gnaw at their bones.

"We gonna talk tonight? Or you still pretendin' I don't exist?" The Maid asks sourly, the fire filtering her voice from sweetness to grating metal.

"I didn't think you were wantin' to talk to me," The Brute admits.

"Better than the silence."

"Alright. What're your interests?"

"What're my interests?"

"That's what I asked, isn't it?"

"I suppose we oughta start somewhere. I like to write and read. Yourself?"

"I ain't got no interests. What you read?"

"Philosophy mainly. A lot of Plato. Read Ovid's Metamorphoses not so long ago."

"Never heard of 'em."

"I can tell."

"What they write about?"

"Myths, mainly. In Metamorphoses, this guy called Orpheus tries to rescue his wife, Eurydice, from The Underworld. He's got this lyre instrument that he plays so beautifully it makes Hades weep. The God of The Underworld allows Orpheus to lead Eurydice back up to Greece but says that Orpheus can't look at her until

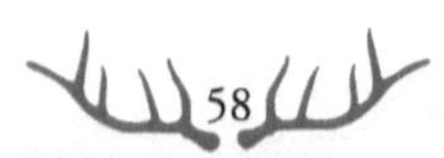

they're both safely alive. And so, he's walkin' Eurydice back to life and then he looks back too early and she vanishes," The Maid says matter of factly, without a hint of emotion. The Brute studies her.

"You believe in all that?"

"Not yet."

"Why not?"

"They're myths. There ain't no heroes or Underworld. We all enjoy pretendin' we're better than we are. Deep down there's nothin'; and after all this, there's nothin' twice fold."

"Why read about it then?"

"Why do little girls play dress up? It's fun to pretend," The Maid states. An owl hoots, the only break from the constant wind shoving against The Brute's back.

"That's a little nihilistic," he replies, finally.

"That's a big word for you … You're right, maybe I just like readin' without thinkin' about what all them words mean."

"You're too young to be thinkin'. Just live a little."

"Is that what you do?"

"No, but it's what I'm telling you to do," The Brute commands.

"That's the only thing you've told me that makes much sense."

"I'm sorry," he mutters with a tremble, stopping the conversation dead in its tracks.

"For what?" She eyes him with wariness.

"Everythin'."

"I should hope so. You done some messed up things." She laughs as she says this and it's a rumbling laugh from deep down in the catacombs of her belly.

The brute smiles, sadly, and says: "I ain't good at talkin' or apologisin' or none o' that shit, but I am sorry. This is all my fault. You should have stayed with the woman, she would've kept you safe." He hopes The Maid will disagree. He wants her to reply with a list

of all the reasons he is good. The ground beneath his arse is littered with stones, he can't get comfortable.

"You know, I saw you the night that it happened," The Maid whispers, seemingly off topic. "All this ash was floatin' in the air, little deadlights my mother called them. We were runnin' but at some point she died, I only knew cause her hand stopped grippin' mine. The mud was slippery, which was strange because you'd think all that heat would dry it up, and I remember falling over in the sludge and hound dogs tearin' past me. Their fur was all matted and they had these spiked collars that were diggin' into their necks, makin' them more vicious. One of em' ate Jimmy the Butcher like he was just a piece of meat, which I guess he was – ironic considerin' his profession.

"Anyways, I was curled up in a ball, hands slammed over my ears, prayin' to god n' mindin' my own business. Then I see you waltzin' out of those shabby stables with three horses in tow, right before the whole buildin' toppled over nonetheless, like some hero. There I am thinkin', here's a brave fella who'll come n' save this helpless, timid, recently made orphan. But then I watch you shove past a burnt up beggar and he shrivels up into a ball and ends up lookin' just like me.

You disappeared into the night with those three horses, next thing I'm stumblin' through smoke. Scariest part was these outlines of people would form and I wouldn't know whether they were good or bad till they were an inch or two away. Luckily, the only people I passed were mothers and children. I made it out of there, came across the others – who are now dead anyways – and three days later we bumped into you at our camping grounds. You were ridin' a stallion, the other two horses were gone." The Maid finishes her tale and reluctantly raises her purple, hazy eyes to glare her way through the cracks in The Brute's heart, into the recesses of his soul.

"Why'd you tell me that?" The Brute asks.

"How do you do it?" She asks, bluntly.

"Do what?"

"You know what." Her lip trembles.

The Brute considers her question. "I try not to think about it."

"Eventually that's gonna stop workin'."

"I know."

"What'll you do when that happens?"

"I'll cross that bridge when it's burnin'."

"I don't think that's the sayin'."

"Does it matter?"

"Do you hate yourself?" The Maid's straightforward question catches The Brute off-guard. He picks at his teeth, chewing on his last remaining piece of tobacco. A destroyed spiderweb is pressed against the velvet fabric of his wide-brimmed hat. "Tell me." The Maid snaps his attention back to her.

"Yeah, I do."

"Why?" she asks.

"Because I'm me. If that ain't enough reason to hate myself I don't know what is." The Brute's being sincere, but something deep in his core still feels off, as though that weren't enough of a response. He hooks his hat onto the branch of a nearby tree and leaves it there.

"I wrote a poem, care to hear it?" The Maid asks.

"Are we talkin' about poems now? I thought I was bad at conversations but 'ere you are barely able to talk about one topic for more than a minute." He sighs, "Go on, then. Let's hear it." The Brute is not one for poetry, but he also does not want the conversation to end. The Maid pulls out a small parchment from her blouse, there seems to be several poems written on there.

"Flower petals sing
Hymns of dead man's burnt down house
Now a poppy field"

The Brute hears her words but can't piece it together into a coherent whole. "Is that it?" He finally asks.

"It's a *haiku*. I thought you might not like it."

"No, I do."

"It's alright. Don't lie. There's always later." And with those words The Maid settles in for the night. Within moments, she's asleep.

The Brute rests his head on a bundle of clothes. He pictures The Girl With Hair Like A Storm dancing in a meadow with her father, but The Maid's words have forced him to question the very real possibility that the Girl is gone. She lived knowing one day she would die, and now she's dead and knows nothing. She's no longer a part of this world, no longer tethered to the land or its people. Even her name is but a word that The Brute will never know.

The sky above is filled with stars, each of which is a man or beast with their own lives, their own dreams. Do stars wage war? Do they love or hate or merely float?

The branches of the trees above, earthbound and yet so distant, connect those dazzling, starry bulbs together; creating pathways to trace with the eye and a map that leads to some faraway realm. Perhaps that realm won't be someplace better but, at the very least, it will be someplace that is not this place. And that, is better than nothing.

ACKNOWLEDGEMENTS

WHERE TO START? I think the obvious place is with Karen Mc-Dermott and the team at Making Magic Happen Press who took a chance on a young writer who knows nothing about writing a novella and published his strange Western story. Thank you, guys, for your support and for taking the risk.

To Dylan Ingram, you're a talent to be reckoned with and the cover you have designed is better than the content inside. Thanks for putting in the effort to illustrate something memorable, eye-catching and artistic.

John Beaton, who I did a screenwriting course with at KSP Writers Centre, if you're seeing this I want to thank you for the tips, strategies and skills that allowed me to actually complete Deer Head. I think the novella is, at the very least, a complete story and that's not due to my capabilities as a writer but because of your guidance (and of course, Mum and Dad's, which brings me to my next group on the big 'thank you' list).

Hello, family. Don't worry, I didn't forget about you. Mum and

Dad, cheers for encouraging me to write. Benson, our family dog, thanks for giving me your moral support with your smile and for taking me on walks around the neighbourhood (walking helps me think of ideas). And Imani, my sister, you didn't really do much but thanks anyways. You're a good sister.

Finally, to my readers; if you're reading the acknowledgements then that means you probably read what I wrote and have enough of an opinion about it to take the time to scan over my acknowledgements. Thanks for reading my work and buying my book because that is one extra dollar in my pocket. And in the end, that's what this is all about. Making money! Muahahaha.

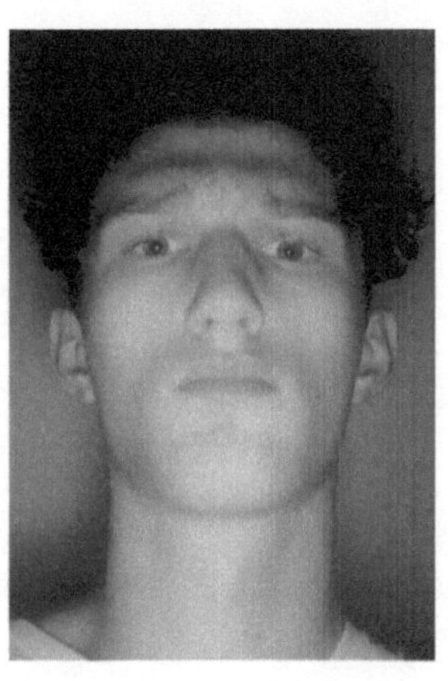

ABOUT THE AUTHOR

KAYIN VAN NELSON IS A seventeen-year-old emerging film director and creative writer. He is the winner of an SHC Young Filmmaker Award and 1st place Write for Fun short story prize winner. He completed a holiday film director course at The Australian Film Television and Radio School in Sydney and a one-year scriptwriting course at the Katharine Susannah Prichard Writers' Centre in Western Australia. Several of his short stories and poems have been published in anthologies. He has also written scripts, directed, edited, and composed music for short films, live shows, author launches and spoken word events, with film reels screened at Melbourne Fringe and Melbourne Spoken Word Festival. In his spare time, he enjoys making wacky animations, relishing in the humour of Bojack Horseman, and becoming invested in the latest story-driven video games.

www.ingramcontent.com/pod-product-compliance
Lightning Source LLC
Chambersburg PA
CBHW030438120726

47903CB00003B/1025